Festive Fantasies

Lyla Andrews

Festive Fantasies: A Christmas Erotica Novella

Copyright © 2023 Lyla Andrews
All rights reserved.
No part of this book may be reproduced in any form without the prior written permission from the author, except in the case of brief quotations in reviews and noncommercial uses permitted by copyright law.

This book is a work of fiction. Any resemblance to actual places, people, or situations are products of the author's imagination and are entirely coincidental.

For any questions, please contact the author at
lylaandrewsauthor@gmail.com

Content Warning

This novella is not suitable for anyone under 18 years of age. It contains sexually explicit content, including the following: unprotected sex, bondage, degradation/humiliation, exhibitionism, CNC, impact play, choking, and the heroine being shared between two men.

CHAPTER ONE

THE BLAST OF cold air bites at my skin as I carefully exit my car and ensure that my heels have a grip on the icy pavement before I fully shift my weight to my feet. The sun has already dipped below the horizon, but the colorful string lights adorning Donovan's house glow like a beacon in the darkness, providing some much-needed cheer to the bleak, wintry atmosphere. I take slow, deliberate steps as I make my way to his door, and despite the cold, my body warms at the thought of seeing him again.

Even though we started dating right after Halloween, we haven't had much time to spend together. After spending almost a week in Florida for Thanksgiving, I got back home only to immediately begin cramming for my finals. Donovan has been incredibly patient, but the stress of sneaking around is already wearing on us both.

When I left the house earlier today, I told my mom and dad that I was spending the weekend with my best girl friends, which they didn't question. Thankfully, they don't have much of an interest in my personal life, but I know I'll have to tell them sooner rather than later about my relationship with Donovan.

I just hope Dad doesn't have a heart attack or commit murder when he realizes that his daughter is secretly dating his best friend. But that's a problem for another day.

I knock on the door, still not quite comfortable with simply letting myself in, and Donovan opens it a second later.

"Hey, beautiful," he greets me, wrapping me in a hug and pulling me into the house. My anxiety immediately melts away as I relax into his warm embrace and inhale the scent of his cologne.

"I missed you," I mutter into his chest.

He smooths a hand over my hair before pulling back. I immediately miss his warmth. His eyes rove over my body, taking in the outfit I spent way too much time figuring out this morning. I wanted to look classy when meeting his friends for the first time, but I also wanted to look sexy for him, so I decided on a long-sleeved green velvet dress that hugs my torso and flares out at the hips. It only reaches a few inches above my knees, but I have on thigh-high stockings that will look like normal tights to everyone else.

Donovan leans down to kiss me, but I only press a chaste kiss to his lips before pulling away. "You're not allowed to mess up my makeup until your friends leave," I tease.

"Oh, I'll hold you to that later," he mutters. I laugh at his feigned pout as I follow him further into the house.

Even though we haven't had as much time together in the past couple months as I'd like, there's already something undeniable between us, more than just the kinky sex that threw us together in the first place (though that definitely doesn't hurt matters). Every moment I've spent with him, he's been kind and attentive, always making sure I'm taken care of not only physically, but emotionally.

One week after our initial meeting on Halloween, I accepted his invitation to come over, nervous about how he might act and if there would be anything more than just sex (though I probably wouldn't have complained then, either).

But to my surprise, he cooked me dinner and had my favorite drink on hand, which he must have remembered from our first night together. We talked late into the night and got to know more about each other, and his softer side began to show more with each subtle moment together. The juxtaposition between his tough, serious demeanor and his gentle actions almost seems too good to be true, but he's continued to prove his sincerity time and time again. In fact, the only time he doesn't treat me gently is when we're fucking, and it has me absolutely addicted to him.

Donovan takes my coat, not-so-subtly brushing his hand across my chest as he pulls it off my shoulders.

"It looks great in here," I tell him. The house has been neat and clean every time I've come over, but he's definitely stepped up the decorating for the party tonight. A pile of unused decorations sits on the dining room table, indicating he isn't quite finished yet. Candles burn on the counter tops, filling the air with the warm scent of vanilla and cinnamon.

He thanks me and casually begins untangling a string of lights on the table. He's never been very talkative, and I'm usually fine with our stretches of comfortable silence, but my anxiety creeps in again and I can't keep myself from speaking.

"I'm nervous to meet your friends," I admit.

He looks up. "Why?"

"I don't know, honestly. I guess I just want to impress them." A thought crosses my mind that makes my heart lurch. "None of them know my parents, do they?" Donovan and my dad do have some friends in common, and the last thing I need is for someone to recognize me and tell my parents about this relationship before I can do damage control.

"No," Donovan says, "though it wouldn't be the end of the world if they did. We're both adults, and I don't want to sneak around like teenagers forever. We have to tell them at some point. I'll deal with the fallout from Conrad if necessary."

I nod. "You're right. I guess I'm just worried about this ending badly if he gets pissed."

Donovan sits on one of the dining room chairs and pulls me onto his lap. "I don't care what happens with him, Zoe. If he accepts it, great. If he doesn't, then fuck him. But anything he might say or do has no bearing on how I feel about you."

His reassuring words ease my fears, at least for now. He places a gentle kiss against my neck and wraps his arm easily around my torso. His fingers graze my waist, and my skin erupts in goosebumps. I melt into him as his hands begin to wander and explore. When his fingertips slip under the hem of my dress and he discovers the top of my thigh-highs, he pauses.

"I like these." His voice is deep and low, his mouth only inches from my ear.

"I thought you might," I respond, grinding my ass into his lap as his fingers trace the bare skin of my thighs.

"Oh, you'll pay for that later," he growls. "But for now, I have something I'd like for you to do." He moves to stand, sliding me off his lap.

Damn.

"And what would that be?" I ask.

He leaves the room only to return a moment later with a piece of paper and a pen in his hand.

Before I have the chance to ask questions, he explains, "I made this list for you to fill out."

"Do I have to check it twice?"

He raises an unimpressed eyebrow at me while I laugh at my own joke.

"Sorry, the joke was right there. I had to say it." I detect the slightest lift of the corner of his lips and a spark of amusement in his eyes, but his serious expression remains mostly unchanged.

"Actually, it probably would be a good idea for you to double check this, probably more than twice," he says with a knowing smirk. *Interesting.*

He hands me the paper, saying, "If you want to do this, we need to do it right. I need to know what you're interested in and what's a hard limit for you."

I glance at the paper, noticing that the list consists of different kinks and sexual scenarios. Next to each item is a scale of 1 to 5, with 1 representing an absolute "no," to 5 representing an absolute "yes." 3 is "unsure/maybe." I'm supposed to mark my preferences in trying each one of these, though thankfully there aren't many items.

"I didn't put everything on there, but those are the ones I'm most curious about. I'm going to get the snacks ready," he says. "Take your time, and be honest." With that, he kisses me and disappears into the kitchen, leaving me alone with my thoughts.

I take a deep breath and read over the list. I've been wondering if we were ever going to do more sexually than we have been, since he insinuated we would after our first night together, but I've been too shy to ask. Of course, we've kept to the basic kinky stuff, like blindfolds and spanking and handcuffs, but aside from that, there hasn't been much . . . exploration. I have, however, done my own research in my free time, so I at least know what most of these terms mean.

Reading through the list, I can't help but wonder if he's only chosen acts he's interested in, or if he provided an array for my sake. Regardless, I slowly make my way through the list, and there are a few times I have to pull out my phone to look up exactly what some of these things mean. With each one, I imagine it playing out in real life with him—or in some of these cases, with others. *Would I want that? How would it make me feel, not only during, but afterward?* I envision myself in these situations, then circle a number based on what reaction it elicits. Most of them excite me, or at least interest me, and my core begins to ache with some of these made-up scenarios playing out in my mind. My willingness to try some of these comes as a surprise—I never thought I'd be the type of girl who's okay with being shared with other men, for example. But when I see it on the list, I find myself circling the number 4 out of both curiosity and surprising excitement, though I do add a note next to it.

"*Only if you'd like it, and only if he's attractive!*" I draw a little winking face next to the note for good measure, then move on down the list.

Exhibitionism? 5.

Objectification? 5.

Forced orgasm? *Definitely* a 5.

In fact, the only thing I mark under a 3 is Anal (1—no way). As much as I can appreciate how so many people seem to enjoy it, it's just never been something I'm into.

I continue down the list until I reach the end, then check it over to be sure of each answer. When Donovan enters the room again, I proudly slide the list across the table to him. His eyes track from top to bottom, evaluating each one, before he gives a satisfactory nod.

"What's the verdict?" I ask flirtatiously. "Naughty or nice?"

He locks eyes with me and shoots me a playful grin, running his fingers through his thick beard. "Very, very naughty." He kisses the top of my head. "And would you be willing to start trying some of this out later tonight?" he asks, his voice calm and steady as he trails his fingers across the nape of my neck, making my skin erupt in goosebumps.

"Yes," I say, probably too quickly and with too much enthusiasm. "Absolutely," I add, calmer this time. I'm eager to do anything and everything with him at this point, but he obviously doesn't seem to mind. We haven't had nearly enough time to experiment yet over the past couple months.

The issue now is that I don't even want to have this little Christmas party he's planned; I want to skip over it and instead spend the night having him all to myself, letting him fuck me in every way imaginable. Of course, I'll enjoy meeting his friends, but now the only thought occupying my mind is, *what is he going to do to me later?*

One thing's for sure: I can't wait to find out.

CHAPTER TWO

DONOVAN AND I spend the next hour finishing decorating and putting out snacks and drinks. Time seems to move in slow motion now that I have something to look forward to once the party's over.

"How many other people are coming?" I ask. He tells me it'll be six to eight of his closer friends, which is fewer than I expected. At least it should be easier to socialize that way.

After I've hung the last decoration in the living room, Donovan motions for me to follow him and sit down. I take a seat at the kitchen table and realize he's holding the list again.

"You're absolutely sure about all of these?" he asks.

"Yes."

"Do I need to explain what any of these mean in any more detail?"

"No." I won't tell him that I've been doing my own research on the internet lately—*porn counts as research in this case, right?*—, so I'm pretty familiar with most of these terms. The ones I didn't know, I looked up while filling out the list.

"Remember that you can use our safe word at any time," he says. He wears a serious expression, more serious than I think I've ever seen him. "It exists for a reason," he continues, "and you should never, ever feel ashamed if you need to use it. I want to reiterate that."

I nod my head. "I understand." But why is he telling me all this now? We still have to spend a few hours around other people, and I have to pretend to not be a needy mess that's just dying to climb on top of him at any given moment.

"Well, then." His demeanor shifts in an instant from concerned to dominant and commanding. "Let's put you to the test. Come with me." I stand from his lap, my heart thumping in my chest, and follow him into the living room, where garland covers the fireplace mantle and multicolored string lights hang around the edges of the room thanks to our concerted effort of decorating. A Christmas tree stands tall and wide, filling the far corner.

I realize that I left one of the kitchen chairs against the wall, as I had used it as a step stool to reach near the ceiling earlier to put up decorations. Donovan seems to notice and walks toward it just as I say, "Sorry, I forgot to put that back earlier. Here, let me move it."

"No need." He moves the chair, sliding it about a foot away from the wall, and adjusts it so it's facing the middle of the room. "Sit," he commands. The strict, authoritative tone of his voice sends a jolt through my spine, and I immediately obey.

I sit in the chair, waiting for him to explain what he's up to, but instead of explaining, he simply leaves the room. *Ooookay then.* A few seconds later, he returns holding more string lights and . . . rope? The rope is thin and red, like the Shibari ropes I've seen online in my "research." *This man sure likes his rope,* I think, fondly remembering our Halloween escapades. Not that I mind . . .

I stay seated, my mind racing as he casually untangles the lights and the rope. Why is he doing this now? It's not like we'll have time to do much before people start arriving, though maybe that's part of the thrill to him. Getting in a risky little quickie or whatever. I don't ask questions, only wait, until he finally speaks again.

"I want you to put your arms on the armrests to your sides," he instructs. I do as he says, and he gently adjusts my arms so that they're directly on top of the thick wood with my elbows tucked back slightly and my forearms lying flat against it. My heart races as he nods approvingly and kneels next to me, caressing my thighs before spreading my legs apart so they're even with the front legs of the chair. The tips of my heels sit parallel against the chair's legs.

When Donovan picks up the rope next to him and begins wrapping it around my leg, I can't hold back the thought running through my head, even though there's already a constant rush of arousal coursing through me after filling out that list and thinking of all the things he could do to me.

"A-aren't we cutting the time a little close?" I manage to ask. "I thought your friends were supposed to be here soon."

He smirks. "They are, and you'll look so pretty on display for all of them to see."

My eyes practically pop out of my head. Did I just hear him right? *Me* on display for his friends, who I've never met? I start to speak and it comes out as an unintelligible stutter. Even *I'm* not sure what I'm trying to say.

"Is that okay, Princess?" He asks, using his nickname for me—the one he gave me on Halloween. Flashbacks of that night flit through my mind: our initial meeting before we knew each other's identities, him chasing me through the woods then fucking me when he caught me, him wrapping his belt around my throat and making me crawl for him . . . I brush away the memories before I let myself get too carried away in them. I'm already in too much trouble, it seems.

I think about the situation I'm currently in—really think about it and how I feel—then nod in response to Donovan's question.

"Use your words, baby," he coaxes.

"Yes," I say. "I'm okay with this." The thought of Donovan wanting to show me off in his own way fills me with warmth and even pride. If he wants me to be on display like this, that means he's proud of my looks, and likely my willingness to participate in his kinky endeavors.

He gives me an encouraging smile and gets to work on tying up my legs with intricate loops that I'm sure will not come undone easily. Meanwhile, I'm already reeling at the thought of absolute strangers seeing me like this. I know I'll spiral trying to think of all the ways this situation could go embarrassingly wrong, so I instead focus on the way Donovan delicately threads the silky rope through his hands and around my body as he binds me to the chair. He works at an easy pace as he carefully loops the rope around my calves before crossing it over my inner thighs and looping it again, this time around my forearms. With each layer he adds, my breath quickens and my skin heats, and I realize I'm already wet, not only from the riskiness of this whole situation, but also from the gentle, lingering touches from Donovan as he works his way around my body, as if I'm a work of art he needs to display perfectly.

With the remainder of the rope, he crosses it over my chest in an intricate star pattern that emphasizes my tits. I look down and realize that, with my legs spread open, the tops of my black thigh-highs are showing and the fabric of my dress falls between my legs rather than flaring out to the side, just barely enough to cover my panties. When I left the house earlier, I thought I looked fairly classy with a subtle hint of sexiness: a long-sleeved dress that doesn't show cleavage, plus tights—or, what looks like tights to everyone else—to make up for the shortness of the flared dress. But now, I look positively sinful, and I'll apparently be on display for all of Donovan's friends to see.

Fuck.

When Donovan stands, grazing his finger over the line of my collarbone as he surveys his work, I test the restraints by pushing and pulling against them. There's absolutely no way I'm getting out. I watch silently as he lifts the end of the string lights and begins to lightly wrap them around my body and the chair as the final piece of the decoration—me. Once they're draped over my shoulders and torso, he plugs them in and the lights come to life, a festive combination of red, green, blue, and yellow. They cast a soft glow on my dress and my skin.

Donovan steps back to survey me and nods approvingly. "Beautiful."

I bite back my smile. "Thank you. You're a good decorator," I tease.

He glances at the clock on the wall, and I follow his line of sight. Only ten minutes until the party arrives. Suddenly, It feels almost impossible to sit still, but I don't exactly have much of a choice. Donovan chuckles as he pulls out a piece of paper from his back pocket and unfolds it. It's the list I filled out earlier.

"So . . ." he starts. The pause before his next words feels like minutes rather than seconds. He opens his mouth to say something but closes it again and shakes his head, as if changing his mind about whatever he was going to say. "Do you trust me?" he asks instead, refolding the paper and shoving it back into his pocket.

"Yes."

He only answers with two words. "Okay, good." No explanation, no details, nothing. He moves toward me and kisses my forehead before leaving the room while my mind is once again left reeling. I take a deep breath to calm myself. I trust him, but I can't help but wonder what else may happen over the course of the next few hours.

He wouldn't knowingly put me in a position that would cause me any legitimate discomfort, I remind myself. If he does something, it'll be because he thinks I'll enjoy it.

"One last thing," Donovan announces when he reenters the room. He holds up an oversized red ribbon, probably four inches wide and close to two feet long.

"What's that for?"

He walks behind me and reaches his arms over my shoulders, putting one end of the ribbon in each hand before bringing the middle over my mouth. I can feel his fingers work as he ties a bow at the back of my head.

So, not only am I unable to move in my vulnerable state, but now, I can't even talk. I'm not sure if that's better or worse, but one thing's for certain: I'm now the most festive decoration in the room, and I can't do much more than the Christmas tree sitting in the other corner with all my limitations.

Donovan rounds the chair and crosses his arms, taking me in with a look of pride and desire.

"You look absolutely fucking perfect," he praises.

My face flushes, his endearment zipping through me like a bolt of electricity. His praise alone already makes this more than worth it.

CHAPTER THREE

BY THE TIME the doorbell rings, my stomach is doing somersaults. What if these people come in and laugh at me? I'm wrapped in string lights with a bow around my head, for Christ's sake. Voices resound down the hallway from the front of the house, but I can't make out what they're saying over the low, steady stream of Christmas music coming from the living room speakers. I make out Donovan's low tone, followed by a chuckle, and wish I could eavesdrop. Shifting in my seat, I try to adjust myself, but there's not much I can do with the rope wrapped around me. I just have to wait here like this, tied up and on display for everyone to see.

My skin heats as footsteps sound down the hallway, coming closer and closer until a group of three rounds the corner, followed closely by Donovan. I can't even give them an awkward wave or say "hi," which somehow makes this even worse.

Two of the people are clearly together—a small, mousy brunette and a tall, heavily tattooed man. His arm is casually wrapped around her waist, and she keeps leaning into his chest. The other man with them is bleach blond and decked out in an ugly Christmas sweater with a penguin pattern covering the entire thing. They all clearly notice me, casting interested glances my way every minute or two as they continue their conversation, but I don't detect any judgment in their eyes. The woman is smiling shyly, and her eyes flick over to me more than anyone else's. I don't know if she envies me or pities me.

"Dylan couldn't make it?" Donovan asks the man in the Christmas sweater.

"Unfortunately not," he answers. "He couldn't get off work."

"That's too bad." The other two echo his sentiment as they all make their way into the kitchen for drinks. Donovan casts an appreciative glance toward me, letting his eyes linger on my exposed thighs for a few seconds just before he rounds the corner.

My stomach knots as they walk away. Is this how it's going to be all night? I definitely don't hate it, but it's going to be a long night if I'm stuck sitting here like an inanimate object for hours on end.

The doorbell rings again, and I train my ears on the excited greetings that burst forth, but I still can't make out anything more than snippets of the conversation.

Again, my body tenses with adrenaline as the new group follows the same path down the hallway, the sound of their footsteps building until they appear in the entryway.

I don't make eye contact. Embarrassment flushes my body as they fall silent.

Even though it's fewer than five seconds of silence, it feels like eternity. Finally, someone speaks up.

"Well, Donovan, I have to say that you really stepped up your decorations this year," a woman says with kind humor in her voice.

"Agreed," one of the men replies. "Fucking beautiful."

I try to fight back the smile that comes to my lips while I brave lifting my gaze to them. Again, it's three people—two men and a woman—but none of them seem to be together from first glance. The woman is tall and thin, with short, dark hair and an air of classy, easy confidence. The man to her side is already in a side conversation with Donovan.

But the other man—the one who spoke—immediately captures my interest. He and Donovan are practically opposites physically—Donovan is broad, burly, and bearded with dark hair and a major intimidation factor, while this man is smaller—though still not small by any means—, with honey blond hair streaked with gray and bright blue eyes that seem to pierce straight into me. There's a wicked gleam in his eyes that makes me squirm in my chair, and the resulting smirk he gives me when he notices my discomfort does something to my body that I can't explain. His attention feels like a spotlight on me. I move to clench my thighs together before realizing I can't. My mouth suddenly feels dry, and I swallow hard, trying to ignore his magnetic presence. From just a few words and his body language, this man exudes charisma and charm.

Who is this man? And why am I having such a reaction to him? Maybe it's because he's the first one to really acknowledge me in this compromising situation I'm in. Not to mention those eyes . . .

Donovan breaks whatever spell I'm under, inviting this half of the group into the kitchen for drinks. They all congregate there, their voices muffled from the wall separating us, and I take a few deep breaths to steady myself. Some people are just charismatic, I tell myself. Nothing to be weird about. I'm sure my senses are just heightened from the thrill of all this, that's all.

Thankfully, the party slowly migrates from the kitchen into the living room. I can't really talk, but I can at least listen to their conversations. Over the course of half an hour or so, I learn who everyone is. The couple's names are Matt and Alondra, and they arrived with Alaric, whose boyfriend wasn't able to join for the night. The second group of people to arrive consisted of Kayla, Lance, and Garrett. From the way they're interacting, it seems that Garrett—the one who I had the intense staredown with earlier—and Donovan have been good friends for a long time.

"Alright, everyone." Donovan's deep voice quiets the room immediately. "I think now's a good time to do the gift exchange." He's met with collective agreement.

Gift exchange? I had no clue about this. Even though I don't know any of Donovan's friends, I can't help but feel a little left out. He could have helped me pick out a gift if it was a random, Secret Santa sort of thing. I suddenly feel like even more of an outsider than I already did. Donovan must notice my frown despite the ribbon over my mouth, because when I catch his eye, his brow is furrowed and he's making his way over to me while everyone else heads into the kitchen to retrieve the gifts they brought.

When he reaches me, he unties the ribbon covering my mouth while everyone else mills about and prepares for opening gifts.

"Don't worry, I didn't forget about you." He opens his large hand to reveal a vibrator—a small one, not much larger than a tube of lipstick—and an accompanying remote. My eyes widen when I realize what's about to happen, and his lips quirk up with a small but devilish smile. I glance behind him at the group of six, but thankfully none of them seem to be paying us much attention . . . yet.

"Don't worry," he says, noting my gaze. "This won't be a surprise to any of them."

"So, did they all know this was going to happen then?"

"Sort of."

His cryptic answer gives me no relief. Did he tell them outright that this was going to happen? Or has this happened before with someone else and they just expect it? The thought of Donovan doing this to anyone besides me sends a bolt of jealousy straight through my chest, so I brush off the thought quickly. Donovan's body hides my small form as he lifts the hem of my dress just enough to slip the vibrator in my panties. It's not even on yet, and I can already tell that this isn't going to be easy. He's situated it so it's rubbing directly against my clit, and my panties are tight enough that they hold it in place against me.

Donovan places a gentle kiss on my forehead before fixing the hem of my dress then standing back up.

"Good luck, Princess," he says with a wicked grin. I watch him walk back to the center of the large room and do my best to stay still. Right now, I need to minimize the friction as much as possible, because if there's one thing I know about Donovan, it's that he doesn't play fair.

I should feel relieved when minutes go by and Donovan doesn't so much as touch the remote in his pocket. But instead, it makes each passing second feel endless. It's like I'm waiting for a bomb to go off at any second, and I know it's coming eventually but with no idea when. And for some reason, that turns me on even more.

I allow myself to get distracted for a moment watching each individual give a gift to another; it's not even a "Secret Santa" sort of thing, I realize, because everyone seems to know who their gift was coming from. Some of them are serious, and some of them are quite the opposite; Matt gifts Donovan a set of nice whiskey glasses, while Alaric gifts Kayla an over-the-top, glittery, double-sided pink dildo that looks long enough to use as a weapon. I don't realize I'm smiling, almost laughing along with them until I'm jolted back to reality by the sudden buzzing of the vibrator. I mutter a string of curses under my breath, which is muffled by the ribbon over my lips, and immediately stiffen, locking eyes with Donovan across the room. I detect the faintest smirk on his lips, but he's otherwise acting like nothing is happening. He turns to Garrett and casually hands him a small box. I can't hear anything they're saying due to the loud, unruly conversations between the others, but they're both smiling and seem to be having a nice time. Meanwhile, I'm doing my best to even out my breathing, to not make any noise. It seems silly to not want to draw attention to myself with the vulnerable situation I'm already in, but for some reason my brain is still set on minimizing embarrassment.

The sense of someone watching me has me looking up again, and I meet the eyes of Garrett, who's sitting right next to Donovan. He lets his gaze linger on the rise and fall of my chest before reluctantly shifting his eyes back to the group. I continue to watch him as he absentmindedly plays with the small box in his hands, his deft fingers weaving through the ribbon.

I wonder what Donovan gave him for a gift. The box is awfully small.

My nerves are on edge and my muscles tight from trying to hold back from moving or making any noise. The pressure is just enough to make me sensitive and needy, but not enough to give me any sort of relief. It's a precarious but infuriating balance. Maybe if I moved my hips against it I'd be able to come, but I refuse to get off from a tiny bullet vibrator in front of seven other people, six of whom I met less than two hours ago. At least, that's what I'm telling myself. Donovan may have other ideas in mind, and I don't exactly have the power to fight.

The vibrations stop suddenly, and I take a deep, relieved breath. Donovan stands seconds later and makes his way over to me, and the butterflies in my stomach take flight. What now?

He leans down so his mouth is inches from my ear, and there's a hint of laughter in his deep voice when he speaks. "Having fun yet?"

I give him a sassy stare but say nothing—partly due to my defiance, but mostly because of the ribbon around my mouth. As if reading my thoughts, Donovan unties the bow behind my head and releases the ribbon.

"I want everyone to see that pretty, pouty little mouth of yours when you're begging me to stop later," he says. And with that, he stands and disappears into the kitchen, leaving my heart pounding and my jaw hanging open.

How far is he going to push me?
There's only one way to find out.

CHAPTER FOUR

WITH NOTHING COVERING my mouth, it's easier for me to breathe now, but it makes my facial expressions much more apparent to everyone else in the room. I take advantage of the vibrator being still at the moment, though I know it could go off again at any second. It keeps me on edge and only halfway able to focus as I listen in on the conversations and watch everyone converse as if I'm not there.

Well, everyone except Garrett. His eyes keep finding mine, and I don't know what it is, but there's something about him that draws me in. Whether it's the devious glimmer in his blue eyes or the subtle smirk on his lips or his smooth, calming voice, I'm not sure.

Reality crashes back to me when Donovan returns to the room. *What am I doing?* I shouldn't be thinking about his friend like this. Is he looking at me a lot? Yeah, sure. But I'm also tied up in bright red rope and covered in Christmas lights like nothing more than a living, breathing ornament, so I'm not exactly a sight one might see every day. If I were him, I'd be staring too.

So why does his gaze more than anyone else's—aside from Donovan's—seem to be affecting me so strongly?

I shake my head gently, as if the action will erase the guilty thoughts from my mind.

As if in punishment, the vibrator in my panties comes to life, this time on higher intensity. A faint whimper falls from my lips, enough to draw attention from more than a few people in the room. My face flushes in embarrassment as I try to keep myself together, but every second that passes makes it more and more difficult. The sheer intensity of the sensation coupled with the fact that I can't move, can't adjust myself, and can't hide makes it almost unbearable to hold back. I notice Donovan in my peripheral vision. He's casually leaning back on the couch, deep in spirited conversation with Garrett as if he's oblivious to the fact that he holds the remote causing me to lose my composure more with every passing second.

I curse him silently as I bite my lip and will myself to not make a sound.

But as I grit my teeth and squeeze my eyes tightly shut, the intensity of the vibrations increases. Every nerve ending in my body alights with pleasure. The sensations travel through my core as I battle for control, desperately trying to remain composed in front of everyone in the room. I want to give into it—to let go and allow myself to feel the release from the need building inside me—but I can't. Not yet.

A moan escapes me, one that I know everyone must have heard. Instantly, Garrett and Donovan's eyes lock with mine. They both wear expressions of amusement mixed with desire, but with the casual way Donovan is still chatting with Garrett while they both watch me gives me pause. He's usually so protective over me, but he doesn't seem to mind his friend watching me struggle against an inevitable orgasm. Interesting.

I begin to writhe against the ropes as I fight a losing battle. The muscles in my legs tighten while I struggle to maintain control, but soon the sensations overwhelm me and I let out a loud gasp. Donovan's grip on the remote tightens at his side as he smirks while Garrett crosses his arms, both of them now totally enthralled with the show I'm giving them.

The orgasm comes quickly, wracking my body and consuming me completely. Tears well in my eyes as I hold back my voice, though small moans and whimpers still escape. The waves of pleasure keep coming, longer and stronger each time until I can barely stand it, my limbs seeming to push and pull against the ropes of their own accord. My blood is pumping so hard I can hear my pulse in my ears, thrumming in time with my throbbing clit.

Finally, the vibrator goes still and the intensity subsides, leaving me panting for breath. Though I've definitely seen a few glances cast my way, nobody is staring at me like I'm the depraved freak I feel like right now.

In this moment I feel completely and utterly exposed. But the way that Donovan and Garrett are looking at me—with unwavering interest and heated stares—dulls the humiliation and embarrassment.

Once I catch my breath, Donovan makes his way over to me and begins untying the rope, gently unwrapping it from my aching limbs.

"You did such a good job, baby," he commends, quiet enough that no one else can hear.

I don't even have the energy to speak back to him. I simply nod before he gingerly helps me to my feet. My legs are shaky, but I manage to stay upright.

"Let's get you something to eat." He wraps an arm around me, and I lean into his side and nod again as he leads me to the kitchen.

He sits with me at the table, making me drink water and have a snack before I can have any alcohol, which is probably for the best. After a few minutes, my energy is back up, even though I'm terrified for how the rest of the evening might go after everyone just saw me become a whimpering, pitiful mess.

"How did you feel about that?" Donovan asks. Concern is etched into his brow, likely due to the fact that I've been mostly silent.

"It was . . . different," I say. "But, I think I liked it. I'm a little embarrassed, but the way you look at me makes it worth it. And I liked the riskiness of it." I won't add that I also enjoyed the way other people, namely Garrett, were looking at me too, though I doubt he'd mind.

He smiles softly and runs his hand back and forth across my upper back in a comforting manner.

"The humiliation aspect is a big part of that," he explains, "but you seemed to have liked that sort of thing before. And you don't need to be embarrassed. None of the people in that room will judge you. I've seen half of them in just as vulnerable situations." He laughs with his last statement, as if remembering one of those times.

"That makes sense," I say. "I guess I'm just not used to being forced to be the center of attention like that."

"Well, you deserve to be the center of attention always. As much as I'd love to keep you to myself, I also love showing off my girl."

My face flushes with the compliment, and I stand to make a drink now that I've finished my water.

Once I've mixed my drink, Donovan escorts me back into the living room. *Play it cool*, I think to myself, preparing for the awkwardness of having to interact with a bunch of people who just watched me come helplessly all over a chair.

But surprisingly, I'm introduced as if I've just arrived, and the conversation flows easily. I make quick friends with Kayla and Alaric, and we drink and laugh into the night while the Christmas music hums in the background. I've forgotten all about my discomfort for now.

My cheeks hurt from smiling as I head into the kitchen to fix another drink. Donovan comes in a few seconds later and sets a box on the counter—the whiskey glasses he got as a gift earlier—then wraps his strong arms around me.

"Having fun?" he asks.

"I'm having so much fun." I grin.

"Good. I told you it would be okay."

I stand on my tiptoes to kiss him, and as we make our way back to the living room, a thought crosses my mind.

"Hey, what did you get for Garrett for his gift? That's the only one I couldn't see."

Donovan slows and looks down at me with a mischievous grin.

"You."

I furrow my brow. "What?"

"You asked me what I got him for a gift. That's your answer: You. You're his gift," he clarifies.

"As in . . ." I trail off.

"Yes," he says. "I figured he'd be attractive enough for you based on those stipulations you gave me on the list."

I swallow hard, taking in what he just told me. Donovan gave Garrett permission to fuck me. I take a deep breath and brace for the onslaught of emotions—fear, anxiety, hesitation—but they don't come. Instead, my whole body seems to come alive with anticipation despite the swarm of questions running through my head. Will Donovan sit back and watch, or will he join? Will Garrett be good in bed? What if I get too nervous and chicken out?

Donovan looks at me for confirmation.

"Okay," I squeak out.

"All you have to do is say the word if you don't want it," he reminds me.

"I know."

With every hour that passes, I think of more ways this scenario could play out, some good and some bad. But despite all my concerns, I do my best to silence my thoughts and enjoy the party while it's still going strong. I'll have plenty of time to deal with this later.

CHAPTER FIVE

I HAVE A few more drinks as the night wears on, but I don't go overboard; it's just enough to ease my nerves while still keeping my wits about me. One by one, people leave the party, and each time the group gets smaller, my anxiety heightens. I hardly know how to act normal now that I know the reason Garrett has had his eyes on me all night.

Of course, anxious as I am, I can't help but feel the tinge of excitement and curiosity that comes with the worry. I'd be lying if I said I didn't find Garrett incredibly attractive, but the only difference from the beginning of the night is now I don't need to feel guilty over it. I find myself peeking at him when he rolls up the sleeves of his button-up shirt, or when he casually drapes an arm across the back of the couch as he's talking. I try to be inconspicuous, but he seems to catch me staring without fail. And every time, my heart seems to stop for a second.

Matt and Alondra are the last to leave, and when the door shuts behind them, it seems to echo in finality. It's just the three of us now, and the tension is palpable despite Donovan and Garrett's continued casual conversation.

My eyes flit between them as they speak, but it's clear from the electric undercurrent between us that we're all thinking about the same thing.

Suddenly, Garrett's piercing gaze is locked on me. "I just want you to know that seeing you tied up like that earlier was the hottest fucking thing I've seen in my life." He says it so smoothly, as if we're talking about something completely normal. But the small changes in his expression—the slight lift of an eyebrow, the curve of his full lips—are enough to emphasize his sentiment.

My cheeks flush with the compliment. How do I even respond to that? "Um, thank you."

"Though," he adds, turning his head toward Donovan, "I think she would've looked even better without that little dress on."

"I agree," Donovan says with a cocky smile. "I figured I'd start her off slow."

That was starting me off slow? This man must be insane.

I stand there silently, fidgeting with my hair and shifting uncomfortably on my feet as they survey me with hungry gazes. There's only a beat of silence before Donovan speaks, jumping right into it.

"Undress her," he commands. I stand there helplessly, my pulse racing and my stomach doing flips.

"It would be my pleasure." Garrett smiles mischievously as he closes the space between us and, to my surprise, kneels in front of me. "I love these," he murmurs, sliding his hands up my thighs and hooking his fingers over the top of my stockings. I take in a sharp breath at the feeling of his fingers tracing down my bare skin as he pulls off my heels then the stockings. I steady myself by grabbing his shoulder as I lift one foot, then the other.

He slowly stands, and even though he's only a few inches taller than me, his easy confidence and flirty attitude make me feel small next to him—fragile, almost—but not in a bad way.

It makes me want even more for him, or Donovan, or both of them to take control of me. I'm not sure if Donovan is joining us or just watching, but his unreadable expression makes me want to do everything in my power to drive him crazy with lust.

Garrett steps behind me and brushes my hair over the front of my shoulder before unzipping the back of my dress. I lock eyes with Donovan as I slip my arms out of the sleeves and let the dress fall to the floor, the fabric pooling at my feet.

His eyes rake over my body as I stand there exposed in only my bra and panties. I resist the urge to cross my arms over my torso. *What now?*

Garrett must also be wondering, because I can sense his hesitation behind me.

"Take the rest off and get on your knees, Princess." Donovan's gruff voice is firm and demanding. My body hums with excitement.

I turn slightly as Garrett takes a step to the side, both of us ensuring Donovan gets a good view from the side, and I gently drop to my knees.

"Suck his cock, baby."

I'm already fumbling with the button on Garrett's pants before he has time to react. He smooths his hand over my hair and says, "You have such a good girl, Donovan."

Arousal floods through me, his praise and the sweet, sultry tone of his voice only spurring me on. He lightly threads his fingers through my hair as I look up at him through my lashes and pull down the hem of his pants. His cock springs free, and I take it into my mouth greedily and without hesitation, hollowing out my cheeks and sucking hard.

Garrett lets out a throaty groan, and I wrap my fingers around the base of his shaft as I take him in my mouth, trying to go deeper with each bob of my head.

"Fuck, that's right," he groans.

I keep my firm grip on him, working him with both my hands and mouth, swirling my tongue around the head as his breathing accelerates. The knowledge that Donovan is watching, that I'm putting on a show for him by sucking off another man, only adds to the intensity. It's absolutely carnal, and sexy as fuck.

"Stop." Donovan's voice isn't loud, but the word rings clear. I slide back, pulling Garrett out of my mouth, the suction making a soft popping sound. My stomach drops with worry for a moment thinking that Donovan has decided he hates this, but when I look at him I don't see any anger or hesitancy in his expression. He's usually somewhat difficult to read, but I'd know that look anywhere; He's just as turned on as I am right now.

I wipe a strand of saliva from my chin, waiting on bated breath for Donovan's next command.

"Come here," he says to me, motioning toward the couch. I move to stand, but he shakes his head. "No, baby. Crawl, just like I taught you." Memories flash through my mind of Halloween night, when he wrapped his belt around my throat and made me crawl down the hallway at his feet. I never thought I'd enjoy something like that, but Donovan has done a lot of things to me that I had never really considered before.

I crawl over to Donovan, not needing to turn around to know that Garrett is watching the sway of my ass as I make my way across the carpet on my hands and knees.

When I get to Donovan, he doesn't say anything, just places his hands on my waist and lifts me onto the couch next to him. He pushes me so I'm lying down with my head on the armrest and my legs across his lap. He trails his warm, rough hands across my body, making me shiver despite the heat. His palms cup my breasts before he pinches my nipples between his fingers, rolling and pinching them just to the point of pain. I cry out at the sensation, lifting my hips in hopes he'll give me some relief.

He doesn't. Instead, he chuckles and stands off the couch, leaving me naked lying on my back. He motions to Garrett and says something in his ear, but I can't hear what. I watch as they walk toward me, taking up places at opposite ends.

Garrett takes a seat on the couch where Donovan had just been, and Donovan stands to the side of the couch by my head.

Wordlessly, Donovan's hands move up to my hair, a soft tug on it makes heat pool between my legs as he pulls the strands out from under my head so they're dangling over the edge of the couch. In one swift motion, he grabs me by the arms and pulls me a few inches closer to him. My head now hangs over the armrest, giving Donovan perfect access to my mouth.

I lift my head momentarily to look at Garrett, who I can feel moving on the couch, though I have no clue what he's doing. Just as I look, he uses his hands to spread my legs, causing one to hang off the couch and pushing the other so it's at the top of the head rest. I'm completely spread and on display for him, and I have a feeling I know what's coming next.

"I can't wait to taste that pretty little cunt," he says, and I practically fall apart hearing those words come from his mouth. The dirty words are such a juxtaposition to his low, soothing voice. Whereas Donovan's voice is rough and deep, almost a growl, Garrett's is silvery and nearly hypnotic.

Garrett dives in, licking me and sucking my clit with such fervor I can't help but cry out. "*Fuuuck!*" My head drops back, and before I can even register what's happening, Donovan's cock is easing into my mouth.

I open wider as Donovan fucks my throat and am unable to hold back my moans as Garrett refuses to let up. The vibration of my moans and hums around Donovan's cock elicits a low groan from him as well.

"That's my girl," he pants as he thrusts into my mouth, my eyes watering as I struggle to catch my breath.

My body is completely overwhelmed with pleasure, and my head is spinning. My moans fill the room, so loud that they nearly drown out Garrett's soft murmurs of appreciation and Donovan's grunts. Garrett's tongue moves in circles around my clit, building up the tension inside me until I'm ready to explode as Donovan pulls out of my mouth and begins stroking himself with his hand.

I lose myself in Garrett's skillful touch, relishing the way his beard scrapes against my inner thighs. He hasn't so much as put a finger inside me, but the way he's licking and sucking and biting is about to push me over the edge. My eyes fall shut as I revel in the feeling, and I listen to the *swish-swish-swish* of Donovan's hand moving up and down his thick cock.

He bends down to whisper in my ear, "Keep your eyes closed and your mouth open, Princess." I nod in response and do my best to follow his instructions despite the onslaught of sensations running through me.

Both of their paces pick up in time with my rapid breaths, and soon, I can't hold back any longer. I come with a shout, waves of pleasure rolling through my body. Garrett moans against my pussy but is unrelenting with his tongue as my hips roll against him. I squeeze his head between my thighs as I cry out, my nails digging into the couch as I clutch at it. At the same time, Donovan lets out a low groan seconds before I feel his hot cum on my face. Drops of the salty liquid hit my tongue as I keep my mouth open, just like he asked, while my orgasm barrels through me.

"Fucking perfect," Donovan remarks.

Garrett finally pulls his face away from me when I'm shaking and coming down from the high. My chest heaves with heavy, tremulous breaths, and I lie still on the couch, unsure of what comes next. I don't know if I could even handle more right now. Garrett looks perfectly at ease, leaning back on his forearm and watching me with interest. He'd almost look casual if his dick wasn't still out and hard as a rock.

I never finished him off, but Donovan stopped us before I could, which means there's probably more in store for the night . . .

At this point, I'm not sure how much more my body can take. I'm usually a one-and-done type of woman, but having the attention of these two seems to have awoken something feral in me. I don't know whether I should feel proud or depraved. Maybe a little bit of both.

Donovan leaves the room and comes back a few seconds later with a washcloth to wipe my face with. Once he finishes wiping my face, I manage to sit up.

"I'll be back," I mutter, standing and going to Donovan's bedroom before either of them has the chance to say anything. There may be more to come tonight, but I need a moment to breathe. I snag one of Donovan's t-shirts from the dresser and slip it over my head, the hem falling closer to my knees than my dress from earlier did. I don't bother putting on underwear; I know they'd be off soon enough anyway.

I return to the kitchen and pour myself a shot of tequila while Donovan gives me a curious glance.

"Doing okay?" he asks.

I cough from the burn of the alcohol coating my throat. "Yep, just need a little liquid courage," I laugh. "I'll be out there in a second."

He gives me a gentle kiss before leaving me alone in the kitchen. I take another small sip of the tequila straight from the bottle and give myself a ridiculous pep talk in my head before taking a deep breath and making my way back into the living room.

"Worn out already?" Garrett teases, taking in the t-shirt hanging from my body like a blanket.

"Maybe, maybe not." I put a little sass in my tone and shrug.

The desire smoldering in his blue eyes intensifies.

"Well, why don't you come on over here then?" he challenges.

I feel like causing a little trouble, just for fun, so I cross my arms over my chest and smirk. "Make me." My attention is so fixed on Garrett that I don't realize Donovan has moved until he's behind me. He steps up behind me and slides his hands around my waist, running his fingers lightly over my stomach. His hard body presses against my back, trapping me in place.

Oops. I'm in trouble now.

"I don't think you realize how easy it would be to *make you*." Donovan's voice is practically a growl as he mocks my words. "But that's okay," he says more casually, looking at Garrett, who takes a step toward me. "She likes it rough anyway." Donovan takes a couple steps backward. "Don't you, baby?"

I nod and bite my lower lip in anticipation.

"How rough?" Garrett cocks an eyebrow and slowly takes a couple more steps toward me. With Donovan behind me blocking the doorway and Garrett moving toward me, I have nowhere else to go. I'm trapped between them.

"As rough as you can give it to her."

Garrett's eyes seem to darken with the challenge. I am *so* fucked, in more ways than one. I think for a brief moment that Garrett may not be the type to get too rough, but it doesn't take more than a few seconds to realize how wrong I am. In one swift motion, he grabs me and twists me around so my back is to him with his hand wrapped around the front of my throat. His long fingers press into the sides of my neck, and I let out a whimper.

Oh. My. God.

Donovan rounds us and settles on the couch to get a better view of us.

"Now fuck her like the pretty little slut she is."

I fucking love the idea of one or both of them using me, the feeling of being totally at their mercy. Even though I know they'd stop in an instant if I said the word, the idea of being outnumbered and powerless against them turns me on in ways I can't describe.

So, I decide to step it up a little more, testing Garrett as much as myself. When his hand leaves my throat and he starts to bend me over one of the low-backed armchairs in a way that will allow Donovan to clearly see my face from the couch, I shoot Donovan a wink as a signal that I'm doing this on purpose before I begin to move.

I push back against Garrett, then attempt to stand and run away. He snatches my wrist and pulls me back into his chest.

"Not so fast, pretty girl," he chides. I feel him hesitate for a fraction of a second until I see Donovan give him a subtle nod in my peripheral vision.

I take the opportunity to push against his chest in an attempt to escape, but he simply chuckles and grabs my wrists, twisting my arms behind my back so my wrists are crossed. He holds them with one hand and shoves me back over the chair, much more forcefully this time.

"Be careful, or I'm going to have to get that pretty red rope back out," he warns, peppering kisses across my neck as he presses his hard length against my ass. The small amount of fabric between us does little to hide his impressive erection.

"Don't threaten me with a good time," I snap back.

I keep fighting back against him as he releases my wrists only to force the oversized shirt off my body, but my attempts are futile. Garrett slips a finger between my legs, feeling the proof of my arousal as I struggle against him.

"You can fight all you want," he says, "but I know you want me to fuck that perfect little pussy. This is all the proof I need right here." He removes his finger from my slit and pushes me further over the chair so my heels are off the floor and I'm balancing precariously on my tiptoes. My balance is thrown off, which makes it difficult for me to move in any way that might have an effect.

Garrett grips one side of my hips with his hand, and I feel the head of his cock nudge my entrance. A gasp lodges in my throat as I attempt to squirm away from his grasp, but to no avail.

"Jesus," he groans as he enters me slowly. "You feel so fucking good." He pushes in and out inch by inch, each thrust stretching me around him until he's seated fully inside me. I gasp at the sensation, especially after having been teased and made to come all night without having anything inside of me. It's been torture in the best way possible. I'm still sensitive from earlier, and that's heightening the experience even more.

Donovan speaks up from across the room. "You're taking his cock so well, baby. That's right, open up for him. Spread that pretty little cunt."

Garrett's hand returns to my neck, his fingers tightening their grip even more, and I let out an embarrassing sort of mewl as he pounds into me from behind. My vision starts to blur and I become lightheaded, my mouth falling open as he hits the spot deep inside of me over and over again.

"You like that?" he asks in a teasing tone, already clearly knowing the answer as he thrusts slowly, rhythmically. The pace is torturous and intense. Every nerve is on fire with the tension building in my body.

I can only nod against his hand. My voice barely sounds like my own as I manage to say one word: "More . . ."

"Hear that Donovan? Your pretty little slut said she wants *more*," he taunts. Donovan wordlessly stands, and from my not-so-great perspective it looks like he's adjusting the string lights over the bookshelf in the corner. He walks toward us with something in his hands, and I don't realize what it is until Garrett's hand moves and Donovan is lifting my torso ever so slightly. It's two of the plastic clothespins we used to secure some of the lights earlier.

Garrett slows his thrusts even more as Donovan flicks my nipples to harden them then clips the clothespins on one at a time. I clench my teeth at the sharp sensation, though every nerve in my body is now on fire. When I lean back down, unable to hold my upper half up for long, the ends of the clothespins rub against the chair, moving them back and forth and pulling my hard nipples along with them.

My whines and whimpers are desperate with each movement, each thrust as Garrett picks up speed again.

"She likes the pain," Donovan taunts, speaking to Garrett as if I'm not there.

"Mmm, that's good." Garrett responds in that charismatic, sultry voice of his. "Does she want more?"

"Y-yes," I breathe. "Please. *Please*."

He hums in approval, leaning closer to me and speaking low. "I love it when you beg. You're just a sweet little fuck toy, aren't you?"

Donovan whispers something to Garrett before returning to his place on the couch. Garrett grabs a fistful of my hair and yanks it back and sideways, turning my head so I'm looking out at the room rather than downward. His touch turns gentle as he brushes the hair out of my face and caresses my cheek. I let my eyes fall closed at the calming feeling, only for it to be replaced a moment later by a sharp, sudden *smack*.

My breathing hitches, my cheek stinging where he just smacked it. A soft moan falls past my lips as he repeats the action, caressing me with his gentle fingers, then hitting my cheek with his palm again. And again. And again.

The overwhelming senses of pain and pleasure have me reeling, and my inner muscles begin to tighten around him and he picks up his pace. Garrett slams into me harder, faster, taking a fistful of my hair again and pulling it back so hard it stings my scalp. Electricity courses through me when I meet Donovan's eyes across the room as I fall apart around another man's cock.

My inner muscles seize as I succumb to the intense orgasm that rocks through me. It comes in waves, rolling through me over and over again until I can barely breathe. I cry out and attempt to rock my hips in time with Garrett's rough thrusts.

"That's it, baby. Come for me. Fuck, you feel so good. *Yes, yes.*" His words are like a chant, spurring me on until I'm falling against the chair in a weepy, shaking mess. As I start to fall back into reality, Garrett reaches his climax with a throaty groan, pulsing and releasing inside me.

After a few moments of silence, the room only filled with the sounds of our labored breathing, Garrett gently wraps his arms around me and pulls me to a standing position, then takes me over to Donovan on the couch. I collapse into the cushions next to him. Garrett leaves the room only to return a couple seconds later, handing me a bottle of water and joining us on the couch.

The soreness is already creeping into my body, and I drink half of the water before closing my eyes and letting myself sink into the cushions. I'm drained, sore, and completely sated. Someone's fingers—I'm not sure whose—comb through my hair, and the gentle, repetitive motions lulls me into a state of exhausted bliss.

CHAPTER SIX

I MUST HAVE fallen asleep, because I slowly come to and realize I've curled up on the couch and have a blanket over me. The men are both still here, talking quietly so they don't wake me. I keep my eyes closed for a few minutes longer, enjoying the contrasted sounds of Donovan's deep timbre and Garrett's soothing tenor.

I could stay here with my eyes closed and listen to them all night, but my daze is interrupted by my need to use the restroom, so I reluctantly sit up and rub my eyes.

"Morning, beautiful," Donovan says.

I give him a sleepy smile. "What time is it?"

"Almost 3 a.m."

"I was just about to leave," Garrett chimes in.

"Well, give me one second and we can walk you out," I say. I'd feel bad if I just let him leave without a word. I run to the bathroom and take care of business, then slip on a pair of sweatpants.

"Thanks again for tonight," Garrett says, putting on his coat. I don't know if he's addressing me, Donovan, or both of us.

"Thank *you*," I reply, and they both laugh.

Donovan claps him on the back and says, "See you again soon, man."

The cold air rushes in as the door opens.

"Well, it was nice to meet you." I awkwardly wave to Garrett as he steps off the porch, talking to him as if he didn't just fuck me to high heaven while my boyfriend watched.

He laughs and waves back before getting into his car and driving away. Donovan closes the door, and the silence in the house seems odd after the wild events of the night.

"So, that really didn't bother you at all?" I ask him as we collapse onto the couch together. Even though I enjoyed myself immensely and will probably be sore for days, I still can't seem to fathom that Donovan would be okay with another man fucking me. It might be hypocritical of me, but if the situation was reversed, I'd probably be heartbroken.

"No, it didn't bother me at all. In fact, I really enjoyed it, if you couldn't tell," he teases. "I loved watching you, seeing everything from another perspective, being able to see your expressions when you're coming so hard taking it from behind—all the while knowing at the end of the night, you belong to me."

I turn and kiss him softly, grateful for his understanding and his willingness to show me things I never would've considered in my wildest dreams otherwise.

He kisses me back, pulling me onto his lap and wrapping his arms around my waist. One hand drifts to my ass and squeezes.

I pull away from his lips. "No offense, but please don't tell me you want to fuck me now too, because I *cannot* handle that after the events that have transpired tonight. Everything might just be numb at this point," I joke.

He laughs as he pulls me into his side. "No, I'm not going to fuck you tonight. Though I have no promises about tomorrow . . ."

I groan sarcastically and bury my head in the crook of his neck.

His chest rumbles with a laugh, and he squeezes me tight against him.

"Merry Christmas, baby."

"Merry Christmas," I repeat with a smile. Three more words are on the tip of my tongue, but I know it's not the right time. I'm sure they'll come out someday soon, but not yet.

I have a very good feeling about him, about us, and I know that this is just the beginning of a much bigger adventure.

Two Weeks Later

I haphazardly toss some clothes into my small suitcase, and my heart feels heavy the more I let myself think.

"It's going to be okay," Donovan promises, "and you can always come back if you need to."

I've been living with him for three weeks now after the debacle of him confronting my father. Donovan had asked him if they could meet at the local coffee shop—a smart move, because my dad cares more about his reputation than anything else, so he'd never cause a scene where other people can hear. Once there, Donovan told him about our relationship and gave him a much more PG-rated version of what happened on Halloween night. My dad was, as expected, absolutely furious and left the coffee shop immediately.

Too add to the hurt, he kicked me out of the house, yelling something about me being ungrateful and fucked up before shutting himself in the office until I left. Of course, I packed a bag and immediately went to Donovan's house, where he comforted me while I cried all night.

Two days ago, my mom—who had been unusually silent throughout the whole thing—called me and begged me to come home, promising that my dad just "needed some time to cool down" and that he regrets going ballistic on me. After talking it over with Donovan, we decided it would be a good idea for me to stay with my parents while I finish college. Classes only started back up a week ago, and it's already been stressful trying to balance everything.

So now, I'm packing my bag as slowly as possible, because I'm dreading going home. Sleeping next to him every night and waking up next to him every morning has been incredible, and I don't want it to end so soon.

"It isn't forever," Donovan assures me. "And like I said, you can always come back, and I'm sure you'll be here most nights anyway."

I nod. "Thank you. And you can bet I will be."

At that, he smiles and pulls me onto the bed with him.

"Every day is one step closer to building our life together," he says. My stomach flutters at the words and the promise they hold. "And I'll be with you every single step of the way."

While You're Here . . .

Want to know the steamy details of Zoe and Donovan's first meeting? Read *Midnight Mischief*! Already read it? Check out the third and final book in the trilogy, *Seduction at Sea*.

As always, thank you for reading! If you enjoyed the story, please consider sharing it with others and leaving a review, as those are the best ways you can support indie authors like myself. I am so incredibly grateful to all of you who have taken a chance on my books. It's still absolutely surreal for me to see people making TikTok, Instagram, and Facebook posts of these dirty little books I've written. I love you all—thank you for being amazing! <3

Other Books by Lyla Andrews

Midnight Mischief (Holiday Heat Book 1)
Seduction at Sea (Holiday Heat Book 3)
Quick Fix
Active
In Between
The Other Side of Summer

Printed in Great Britain
by Amazon